To Dynesti
Love Author Reea Ratney

JUNiPER
AND
ROSE
SISTERS FIRST
AND BEST FRIENDS FOREVER

WRITTEN BY
REEA RODNEY

ILLUSTRATED BY
ALEXANDRA GOLD

Printed in the United States of America.
ISBN-13: 978-0997505900
ISBN-10:0997505907

I would like to dedicate this book to
Emma and Alexa Goldstein, twin sisters
who are the inspiration behind this book.

Also, a special thank you to Susan Goldstein,
their grandmother, for believing in me
and for encouraging me to self-publish
Juniper and Rose:
Sisters First and Best Friends Forever.

And to my two wonderful children,
Denifa and Doreion, whom I love dearly.

Juniper and Rose are beautiful and playful twins.
They do not look alike,
but they are twin sisters all the same.

Juniper has dark shiny hair, big brown eyes,
and a smile that could light up the sky.
She looks just like her mommy!

Rose has red curly hair, hazel eyes,
and a nose sprinkled with the cutest freckles.
Rose definitely looks like her daddy!

Juniper and Rose love each other very much.
Since the day they were born,
they have been together all the time,
and they both seem to love the same things.

They love riding their bikes at the park
on the weekends with their mom and dad.
They love swinging on the monkey bars.

They also love going down the slide and
circling 'round and 'round on the merry-go-round.
They could do that for hours!

The girls have very creative minds.
They especially love dressing up as
fairy princesses and having fancy tea parties
with their imaginary friends.

Their favorite colors are pink and green.
Juniper always wants to wear the pink
princess dress, and Rose always wants
the green one.

They love caring for others, too.
Because of this, their mom and dad call them
the "twin doctors."

Whenever someone is sick,
they are always ready with their first aid kits
and are able to find a cure to save the day!

Juniper and Rose also get into a lot of trouble together. Juniper is known for being the mastermind behind it all.

One day, the girls took colorful markers and drew all over their bedroom walls.
When their mom walked into their room, she was shocked beyond belief!
"Your room!" she said and folded her arms to show her disapproval. "WHAT HAVE YOU DONE?"

With an innocent smile on her lips,
Rose said, "Look, Mom!
We drew a beautiful rainbow just for you!"
Juniper chimed in and exclaimed,
"Don't you love the colors, Mommy? They are just like the ones in the rainbow song!"

Their mother unfolded her arms and smiled.
"You girls will be helping me clean these walls
as soon as you are done, understand?"

They were so full of fun and mischief,
it was hard to be angry with them for too long.

Juniper and Rose once hid their dad's car keys,
so he couldn't go to work.

They giggled as they watched their dad
look everywhere for his keys.

"WHERE ARE MY CAR KEYS?" he asked.
The girls stopped giggling as soon as
he got closer to them.

"Juniper?" He gave a questioning glare in
Juniper's direction.
"Rose?" he asked, looking at her.
"Have either of you seen my keys?"
The girls shrugged their shoulders, smiled shyly,
and at the very same time replied, "No, Daddy."

As soon as their dad walked away,
each twin put a hand over their mouth
and began giggling again.
It wasn't long before they decided to give
their dad the car keys and a big hug.

It didn't matter what they did, naughty or nice.
It was all for one and one for all–sisters first
and best friends forever! That was their motto.
But as Juniper and Rose grew older,
they started to like different things.
That is when it all began–DOUBLE TROUBLE!

Juniper's favorite color was now purple, and Rose couldn't understand why she didn't like pink or green anymore.

Juniper began painting her nails purple. She also had a purple watch, many purple headbands, and she even wore purple lip gloss!

Rose still loved the colors pink and green. She kept all the pink and green things that she once shared with Juniper. After all, pink and green had been their favorite colors all their lives.

Now, whenever they played dress-up,
Juniper wanted to be a mean witch
instead of a fairy princess.
She would often let her imagination run wild
by casting evil spells on their imaginary friends.

Sometimes, Rose would get upset and
call for their mom to make her stop, but
Juniper could be very stubborn. She would not
change her mind about being a witch.

As much as it was difficult for Rose to accept the new Juniper, she was going through some changes of her own.

She no longer wanted to ride her bike at the park. Instead, she would rather sit beneath a shady tree and doodle in her notepad with her markers.

The twins were no longer a team—all for one and one for all, sisters first and best friends forever. They started to drift apart. They couldn't accept the fact that they were both changing.

Their togetherness had started to disappear. Suddenly, the once very happy sisters became very sad little girls.

One night during dinner, it was clear to their mom and dad that something wasn't right. Neither girls touched their meals nor did they speak.

"What's the matter?" their dad asked.

Rose stood up and walked toward her dad.
In a sad, soft voice she replied,
"Juniper doesn't like the colors pink and
green anymore, Daddy.
Her favorite color is now purple.
Whenever we play dress-up and
have tea parties with our imaginary friends,
Juniper wants to be a mean witch
instead of a fairy princess.
She even casts spells on our guests!"

Then with much sadness Juniper said,
"Rose doesn't want to ride her bike with me anymore.
All she wants to do is sit beneath a tree and
doodle in her notepad."

At that moment, their mom and dad
finally realized what was happening.
Their beautiful twin daughters were changing,
and they were having trouble adjusting to it.
They knew this was the perfect time to explain to
their girls exactly what was happening between them.

"You know, girls," their dad said,
"sometimes people change, but that doesn't mean
the love they have for each other is gone."

"But it feels like everything has changed,"
Juniper cried. "How can we love each other
when all we do is fight all day long?"

"Change changes EVERYTHING!"
Rose exclaimed, bursting into tears.

"Not EVERYTHING has changed," their dad replied,
sitting each girl on his lap and kissing them
both on the cheek.

"You still love doing the same things, but in different ways. You both love going to the park, dressing up, and playing with your imaginary friends, and you both love to paint your nails, wear lip gloss, and many other things as well."

Their mom smiled as she recited their favorite motto back to them, "All for one and one for all, sisters first and best friends forever!"

The girls looked at each other and smiled as their mom finished the motto.

"You're right!" they both cheered. "Mom and Dad, you're the best! You saved the day."

"Hey, we said that together!" Rose giggled. "I guess not everything has changed." Juniper laughed.

The girls then thought long and hard
about what their parents had said to them.
Soon they came up with a plan they called
"Teamwork!"

Ever since that day, they take turns painting
their nails in each other's favorite color.
At the park, they take turns riding their bikes
and doodling in their notepads.
Whenever they play dress-up with their
imaginary friends, they both are witches.

Juniper is the mean witch,
and Rose is the good witch.

As the good witch, Rose cast a magical spell
that turns the both of them to
fairy princesses at the end.

Juniper and Rose are on their way
to being the best team ever!

69484554R10024